Reiko's Team

Written by Megan Borgert-Spaniol

Illustrated by Mette Engell

GRL Consultants, Diane Craig and Monica Marx, Certified Literacy Specialists

Lerner Publications ◆ Minneapolis

Lerner Publications Company
An imprint of Lerner Publishing Group, Inc.
241 First Avenue North
Minneapolis, MN 55401 USA

For reading levels and more information, look up this title at www.lernerbooks.com.

Main body text set in Mikado 24/41
Typeface provided by Hannes von Doehren.

The images in this book are used with the permission of: Mette Engell

Library of Congress Cataloging-in-Publication Data

Names: Borgert-Spaniol, Megan, 1989- author. | Engell, Mette, illustrator.
Title: Reiko's team / Megan Borgert-Spaniol, Mette Engell.
Description: Minneapolis : Lerner Publications, [2022] | Series: Be a good sport (pull ahead readers people smarts - fiction) | Includes index. | Audience: Ages 4–7 | Audience: Grades K–1 | Summary: "Reiko is the goalie for her soccer team. By being a good teammate, she helps her team score! Pairs with the nonfiction title Being a Good Teammate"— Provided by publisher.
Identifiers: LCCN 2021010478 (print) | LCCN 2021010479 (ebook) | ISBN 9781728440996 (library binding) | ISBN 9781728444352 (ebook)
Subjects: LCSH: Sportsmanship—Juvenile literature. | Soccer—Juvenile literature.
Classification: LCC GV706.3 .B675 2022 (print) | LCC GV706.3 (ebook) | DDC 796.334—dc23

LC record available at https://lccn.loc.gov/2021010478
LC ebook record available at https://lccn.loc.gov/2021010479

Manufactured in the United States of America
1 – CG – 12/15/21

Table of Contents

Reiko's Team 4

Did You See It? 16

Index 16

Reiko's Team

Reiko gives the ball
to her teammate.

Reiko throws the ball
to her teammate.

Reiko passes the ball
to her teammate.

Reiko rolls the ball
to her teammate.

Reiko kicks the ball
to her teammate.

Reiko's team wins!

Can you think of a time when you were a good teammate?

Did You See It?

ball

goal

tree

Index

ball, 4, 6, 8, 10, 12

give, 4

kick, 12

pass, 8

roll, 10

throw, 6

win, 14